# Kylie Gets a Cochlear Implant

by
## Marilyn C. Rose

## Illustrations by
## Kalpart

D1510848

Strategic Book Publishing and Rights Co.

Strategic Book Publishing and Rights Co.
12620 FM 1960, Suite A4-507
Houston, TX 77065
www.sbpra.com

ISBN: 978-1-62516-170-3

**DEDICATION:**

*I would like to dedicate this book to my husband Marc, and my three sons, Jay, Evan, and Ryan, for always believing in me and giving me the courage!  And in memory of my brother, Martin, who would have been so proud of his little sister.*

# Meet Kylie

Once there lived an eight-year-old girl who was very unhappy. "How can someone be unhappy at the age of eight?" you might ask, "when there are so many interesting things to do, when you do not have to study difficult subjects at school, and when you spend the whole summer with the best grandma in the world eating fruits and playing with your favorite dog?" But Kylie was indeed unhappy because she could not enjoy even a half of those pleasures that ordinary kids usually enjoy. Kylie was deaf. It was not that she could not hear at all, but a person who wanted her to hear something had to scream that something very, very loudly. The thing which made Kylie even more unhappy was that she was not deaf from birth.

Kylie used to hear well when she was younger. She even used to play the piano, and her teacher told her more than once that she could become a talented pianist. Kylie liked the piano and she loved music. She loved singing all those children's songs together with her mom, and she loved dancing. Oh, dancing . . . perhaps she loved it most of all. "When I go to school, I will start taking dancing classes at once," she used to tell her mom at the age of five, "because I want to be like all those pretty ladies in fancy dresses who I watch so often on the TV." Kylie loved TV shows where dancing pairs were competing with each other. She adored the girls' bright and shining dancing suits and even knew the names of all those dances, such as waltz, tango, foxtrot, rumba, paso doble, cha-cha-cha, and many, many others.

Tango

Foxtrot

Waltz

Posodoble

Cha-cha-cha

Rumba

But at the age of six Kylie fell ill with the flu. She never was one of those ailing kids who used to fall ill every winter and every summer after they ate too much ice cream. She just caught that flu somewhere and in a day she was already lying in her bed watching her mom take her temperature. "It's still too high, dear. I think we really have to call the doctor," said Mom anxiously. She asked Kylie's dad to bring her the phone book. Kylie did not like doctors, mostly because she hated to be ill. However, this time she was too weak to argue with her mother. This is why she was simply lying in her bed, waiting for Dr. Anderson, their district pediatrician.

"Yes, it's the flu, my darling," said Dr. Anderson, taking off her glasses and wiping them with a pink hanky. "It is not very dangerous, but you have to stay in bed for at least a week. Drink cranberry juice and take all the medicine that your mom gives to you. I'm almost sure that in ten days you will be playing with your friends again."

Ten days passed but Kylie was still feeling sick. Her temperature did not want to go down and her ears started hurting, as if the

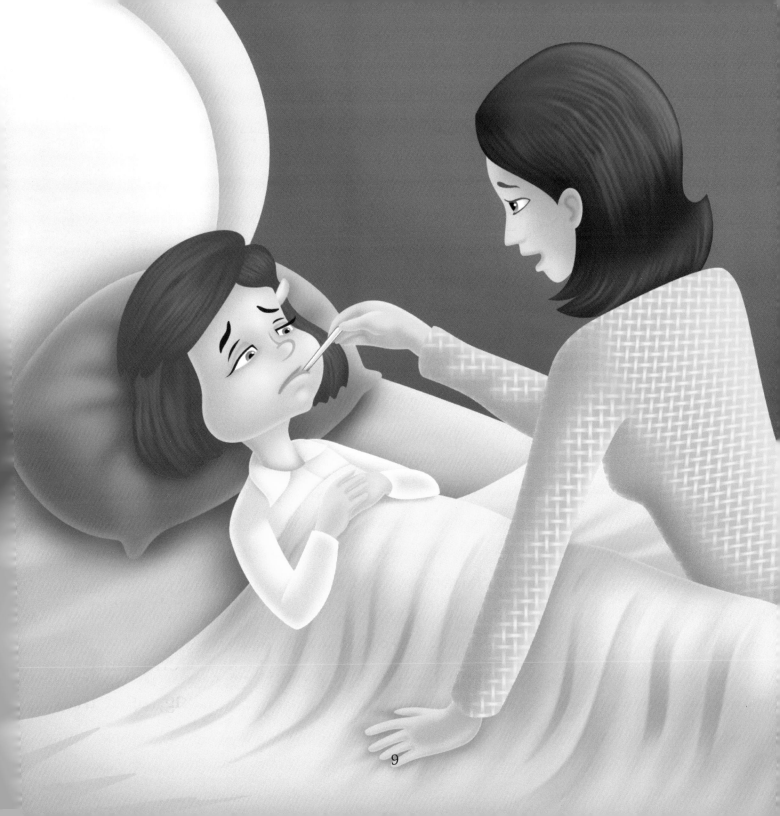

terrible headache was not enough. Now Daddy took her to the hospital himself. The doctor took all the necessary tests and asked for Kylie's father to go out of the ward, for he wanted to talk with him. Kylie watched her father through the glass window in the ward. He appeared to be becoming more and more confused and frightened, as if he was being asked a difficult question and did not know what to answer. In several minutes, Kylie understood why her father looked so puzzled. She was told that she had some kind of aural infection, which progressed very quickly. That infection caused the pain in her ears, but they got to the hospital too late. All that the doctors could do now was to give her some painkillers and antibiotics to relieve her pain and to prevent the infection from spreading further. Then the doctor told Kylie what she was afraid to hear most of all. "You will lose your hearing ability soon. This did not happen yet because the cochlea affected by the infection was not completely ruined and . . ."

Kylie did not want to listen further, mostly because the doctor started speaking with words she could hardly understand. She heard that "sensorineural hearing loss is the most common type of hearing loss" and that it "occurs when there is damage to the peripheral neural end organ", and that people who had the flu and were unlucky to cure it in time had "cochlear pathology." *What are all those weird words for?* wondered Kylie. *I don't understand them and very soon I won't be able even to hear them.*

The next morning Kylie woke up because somebody was touching her shoulder. This was when she understood that the doctor was saying the truth, for she saw her mom's lips moving but could not hear a word.

# A Visit to the Doctor

Two years passed and Kylie got used to her deafness. She learned to lip read and to "speak" with signs, and her parents learned to understand those signs. She began visiting a special school for children with hearing disabilities where there were kids who were either born deaf or who lost their hearing ability because of some diseases—the names of which were completely unknown to her. Kylie could not say that she did not enjoy studying at that school. The class was pretty small and all the kids were got along well with each other. She had some friends who came to visit her at home—though rarely—and whom she visited as well. But Kylie always felt that she did not belong to their world. And she felt that there was something missing in her life.

Her desire to dance grew every day, but even when she turned on the music to the maximum volume, she still could not hear well enough to feel the rhythm. There were dancing classes at the school for deaf children, but what the kids were taught there could hardly be named dancing. They were jumping and turning around in the same place, while the teacher was showing them what to do and pretended to beat the rhythm with her hands. That was not dancing! And Kylie knew that like no one else. In her dreams, she saw herself moving gracefully together with her dancing partner in a beautiful waltz. She HEARD amazing music and she enjoyed listening to it . . . at least in her dreams. Kylie never gave up hope that she would be able to hear some day.

She read in the newspapers that the medicine was progressing all the time and that the doctors started treating even cancer. *What is so special about my disease?* Kylie kept wondering. *Is it more terrible than cancer? Why can't the doctors make something up?*

Then there came a day that changed everything. Kylie remembered well that it on a Friday, because she came back from classes and was sitting on her bed trying to plan her weekend. She did not usually do much on the weekends or Friday evenings. She would be glad to go to the movie, to the circus, or even to the piano concert, but she couldn't. So, most of her weekends were spent reading books and watching cartoons or films with subtitles designed specially for people with hearing disabilities. But that Friday was the most amazing day of all, the day which she would never forget.

Kylie was sitting at the windowsill watching two sparrows trying to share a piece of cookie that she had thrown to them, when she felt her mom gently patting her on the back. She turned around and smiled to her. From her mother's face, Kylie understood that she had some news, good news. And then Mom told her (well, she did not actually tell this, she showed it with gestures, but this does not matter!) that Dr. McMillan, Kylie's otolaryngologist (as Kylie found out two years ago, this doctor treats throat, nose, and ear diseases), called in the morning and scheduled an appointment for them the next day. *What is that appointment for?* wondered

Kylie. "We were at the doctor's two months ago and he told that I was all right. Mom, is anything wrong with me?" asked Kylie.

"No, dear, you're all right. Dr. McMillan said that he had good news for us, so I don't think that it's something about your health," said the mother as she hugged Kylie. "He is waiting for us tomorrow at 11:00 a.m."

The next morning, Kylie woke up earlier than usual. She lay in the bed in that sweet anticipation which children usually feel on the day of their birthday. *Birthday . . .* thought Kylie. *I haven't heard the birthday song for two years. The cake is not that delicious without it, I should admit.* She looked at the window and saw that the sun was shining brightly, the sky was absolutely clear and, as Kylie could only guess, the birds were singing their songs, enjoying the gorgeous weather. It was a beautiful warm May day when nature is usually completely awakened, when occasional rains are not serious at all, and when everybody waits for summer so they can go on vacation.

Kylie dressed herself and quickly ran down the stairs, and saw her mother making breakfast. Though she wasn't hungry at all, her mother still made her have toast and a cup of milk. Afterward Kylie, her mom and her dad finally got into the car and left for the hospital.

Dr. McMillan met Kylie with his ordinary smile, which seemed to never leave his face. He worked with kids only and *Maybe this is why,* thought Kylie, *he is smiling all the time.*

"Do the grownups think that kids like them more when they smile?" Kylie asked her mother once.

"I think so. Isn't it true?" asked Mom back.

"Well, I'm not sure. As for me, I start feeling like I look funny or something. I don't do anything for Dr. McMillan to smile at me like that, so why does he do it?" Kylie kept asking.

"He is just trying to be nice, dear, and that's all," said Mom and (that's unbelievable!) SMILED at her.

The doctor started examining Kylie's ears first and asking whether she ever felt pain or whether there was anything that worried her.

On hearing from her mom that Kylie never complained about that, he nodded approvingly and went to his desk to pick up a magazine.

Kylie saw a smiling girl on the cover of the magazine. The girl could not be older than ten and she looked pretty happy. She was pointing with her finger at her left ear and the heading on the cover ran: "I have got one and what about you?"

*What about me?* thought Kylie. *What should I have got?*

She took another look at the picture but still could not grasp the meaning of it. Dr. McMillan seemed to have read her thoughts, or maybe he just understood from the expression on Kylie's face that she was puzzled. He turned to Kylie's mother and started thoroughly explaining everything to her. The fact that he was not addressing Kylie directly made her nervous and even a little bit angry, but when she tried to lip read Dr. McMillan's speech, she understood why he preferred talking to her mother.

Kylie used to think that she was perfect at lip reading because she could even watch the movies and news reports without subtitles.

It took her some time and effort to acquire those skills, but she always had plenty of time, and was happy to have something to apply her efforts to.

Kylie never found it interesting to play with other kids outside, mostly because they did not find it interesting to play with her. Since none of her classmates lived in her neighborhood, she rarely communicated with other children, except at school. This is why practicing lip reading was one of her favorite pastimes. She also wanted to be perfect in lip reading because she knew that there were not so many people who could do it, and sometimes she was even proud that she could.

So, Kylie could not lip read Dr. McMillan's speech because he was talking in words practically unknown to her. She recollected the day when the doctor in the hospital explained to her the causes of her aural infection in all those weird words. Kylie could swear that she again distinguished something like "cochlear" and "sensorineural," though she could not quite understand what those words meant. Finally, the doctor turned to her and, not surprisingly, smiled pleasantly. Her mom came closer and started speaking slowly and distinctly, trying to explain to her what she had just heard from the doctor. Mom's happy look comforted Kylie a little, though she still could not stop thinking about that funny word "cochlear." From what Mom said, Kylie only understood that some kind of device could help her hear again.

This was all that she needed to know, and as soon as she distinguished from her mom's speech the words "hear again," she asked her to stop and took the magazine from her hands. The title stated that the article about the girl on the cover was on page 7. Kylie opened the magazine and started reading. The article was telling the story of the girl on the cover. It ran:

### Alice Can Now Hear the Rain

*Alice, aged 10, suffered from cochlear pathology* (Here it is again! *thought Kylie) which developed after scarlet fever the girl had when she was 7. The pathology resulted in a hearing disability and spoiled the life of a little girl forever, or as it seemed to be back then.*

Today Alice had the chance to test a cochlear implant, "a device that is partially implanted into the cochlea to directly stimulate the auditory nerve". These implants were first designed in the 1970s, but were improved for use by adults in the 1990s. Such devices were approved to be used by children as well, but around the year 2000 deaf people protested against their application because the implants hindered the children's acquisition of sign language. They believed that forcing deaf children to use these devices deprived children of the freedom of choice.

(Then followed a detailed description of the cochlear implant and the way it works. Kylie chose to skip this part, for it was boring and impossible to understand).

Alice was in the group of kids who tested the implants designed especially for children with her kind of hearing disability. Our correspondent presents an interview with the girl who has not been been talking for almost three years.

"Alice, can you hear me?"

"Perfectly," smiles the girl.

*"Great! Now tell me, how do you feel now that your hearing ability has returned to you?"*

*"Well," starts the girl, evidently trying to pick up words. "How would you feel if you lost something that you liked and missed very much and then it returned to you in three years?"*

*"Oh, what a bright example! I don't know . . . I would probably be the happiest person in the world!"*

*"That's how I feel now," answers Alice, smiling again.*

This is where Kylie stopped reading and raised her eyes at her mother, unable to believe what she just read.

"Can I get one too, Mom?" she asked, feeling that her heart started beating faster than it ever had.

"Of course, dear! This is what the doctor called us for!" answered Mom, and Kylie saw tears glittering in her eyes.

# Getting an Implant

This is was the first time in Kylie's life that she had been waiting for Saturday so much. *A whole week!* she thought. *This is so long! Why should we wait for so long?* But Dr. McMillan strictly recommended doing some tests before getting the cochlear implant. Kylie did not have to go to school for this period of time because, as the doctor said, she needed rest. This was in some way connected with her nervous system and—Kylie did not understand how, though the doctor explained this to her—could influence her future hearing ability.

Anyway, staying at home was even more intolerable, for the days were dragging on unbelievably slowly. There was absolutely no wonder in that, because Kylie was simply sitting in her room and waiting for Saturday. Perhaps especially unbearable was Friday, which seemed to have lasted for the whole week. Dr. McMillan

called in the morning and told Kylie's mom that her tests were all right and that she was allowed to use the implant. "The implant has already been delivered to the hospital," said Dr. McMillan to Kylie's mother, "but you can get it tomorrow because the doctor who will be assisting me will arrive late tonight."

"Was that Dr. McMillan, Mom?" asked Kylie entering the room and seeing her mom put the phone down.

"Yes, we will see him tomorrow morning, dear, at nine o'clock. Would you like some milk?" asked Mom.

"No, thank you," showed Kylie with signs. "I'm ready to go to bed.

"So early?" Mom looked surprised. "It's only half past seven! You've never gone to bed at this time."

"I'm tired, Mommy," said Kylie, pretending to yawn.

To tell the truth, Kylie was not tired at all. She just thought that if she went to bed earlier, the morning would come faster.

And it really did. Though Kylie woke up at 6:00 a.m., she found her mom in the kitchen already and wondered when she woke up. *Maybe she didn't even go to bed,* she thought, because she knew that Mom was also worried about this visit to the doctor.

They had breakfast and even watched cartoons together. Finally, Kylie's father came down the stairs, had his coffee, and told everyone to dress up. "Nine o'clock, nine o'clock . . . ." Kylie could not stop repeating this to herself, for this was when they had to be at the hospital.

They arrived in time and entered the doctor's office at 9:00 a.m. sharp. Dr. McMillan greeted them with his usual smile and met Kylie with his assistant, Ms. Spellman, a young, pretty lady whom Kylie liked at once. Everything else happened so fast that Kylie couldn't even remember it afterwards. Ms. Spellman showed her a little box with that device—the cochlear implant. Then she unpacked it and examined it thoroughly, after which she showed Kylie with signs to come up closer. Kylie could hardly move and breathe; she was so worried. She was afraid that the device wouldn't work with her and this is why she was very nervous.

But it did. In a moment, Kylie's head filled with various sounds. She heard the banging of a door somewhere in the distance, people

walking down the hall of the hospital, cars driving on the street, birds singing, and even the leaves of the trees rustling. But among all these noises, she distinguished her mom's quiet sobbing. She turned around and said aloud, hardly recognizing her own voice, "Mom, it works!" And this was the first time Kylie saw somebody crying from happiness.

In a few minutes, Kylie heard Ms. Spellman talking to her.

"Kylie, Dr. McMillan told me that you liked dancing," she started.

"Why 'liked'?" Kylie interrupted her. "I still do!"

"Of course, you do," smiled Ms. Spellman, even more pleasantly than Dr. McMillan. "My son takes dancing classes at Ms. Finnegan's school and he likes it a lot. I thought maybe you would like to take them together with him. You've missed much, but I'm sure that you will be able to catch up with the rest of children."

"Oh, I will, I will be able!" cried Kylie aloud and began to jump with excitement.

The next day she met Ms. Finnegan, who looked like the girl from those TV shows, and Jason Spellman, who became her dancing partner.

# Bibliography

Dugan, Marcia. *Living with Hearing Loss*. Washington, DC: Gallaudet University Press, 2003.

Mladenovic, Jeanette. *Primary Care Secrets*. London: Elsevier Health Sciences, 2003.

Rubin, Richard, Carolyn Voss, Daniel Derksen, Ronald Quenzer, Ann Gateley. *Medicine: a Primary Care Approach*. London: Elsevier Health Sciences, 1996.

CPSIA information can be obtained at www.ICGtesting.com
Printed in the USA
LVIW01n0209260315
431936LV00009B/71